The White Feather

By Ruth Eitzen

Pictures by Allan Eitzen

HERALD PRESS
Scottdale, Pennsylvania
Kitchener, Ontario
1987

Library of Congress Cataloging-in-Publication Data

Eitzen, Ruth.
  The white feather.

  Summary: A Quaker family living in Ohio in the
1800's makes peace with a Shawnee Indian tribe during
a very troubled time.
    1. Ohio—History—1787-1865—Juvenile fiction.
[1. Ohio—History—1787-1865—Fiction.   2. Quakers—
Fiction.   3. Shawnee Indians—Fiction.   4. Indians
of North America—Fiction]   I. Eitzen, Allan, ill.
II. Title.
PZ7.E347Wh   1987   [Fic]   86-31786
ISBN 0-8361-3439-7

THE WHITE FEATHER
Copyright © 1987 by Herald Press, Scottdale, Pa. 15683
    Published simultaneously in Canada by Herald Press,
    Kitchener, Ont. N2G 4M5. All rights reserved.
Library of Congress Catalog Card Number: 86-31786
International Standard Book Number: 0-8361-3439-7
Printed in the United States of America
Design by Ruth Eitzen

93 92 91 90 89 88 87 10 9 8 7 6 5 4 3 2 1

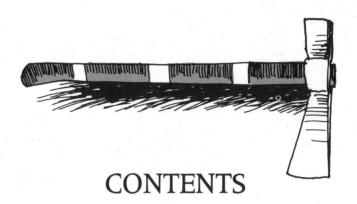

CONTENTS

Chapter One
Indians on the Warpath

Evan, Abe, and Sarie looked down
the mountain at the Ohio River
sparkling in the sun.
A covered wagon was crossing on the ferry,
but it was going the wrong way.
It was leaving the settlement.
Just a year ago, they themselves had
crossed the river, two families in their
two covered wagons, coming *this* way.

5

They would never forget that journey.
They had rumbled along forest trails
and floated at last across the wide river.
They had come here and built new homes
on the edge of the wilderness.
Now Evan's arms were covered
with scratches. Abe's pants were torn.
Sarie's face was purple as a raspberry.
But what did that matter?
It was a sunny summer afternoon and their
berry baskets were almost full.
Wild raspberries hung everywhere like
beads on their silvery stalks.
Since morning the children
had been picking raspberries at the
edge of the forest.
Sarie, Abe's little sister, dropped a

fistful of squashed berries into his basket.
"You look like an Indian on the warpath,
Sarie," Evan laughed. It gave him an idea.
Nearby, the children's mothers were too
busy to pay much attention. The soft blur
of their talking blended with the sound
of the flowing river far below.

The mothers noticed that it had
become very quiet.
Too quiet. Where were the children?
"Evan?"
"Abe! Sarie!"
They called, but there was no answer.
Suddenly a wild, high whoop blasted
the quiet morning.
"Wa-a-a-a-a-a-wa-OOOOOOOOOOOO!"
The two women's faces jerked toward the
dreaded sound of an Indian war cry.
Pale with horror, they stared at the place

where they had last seen the children.

All was still.

Only the leaves moved.

Abe, Sarie, and Evan were gone.

"Ha! We fooled you that time!"

shouted the children, jumping up

from behind the brambles.

Their faces were painted raspberry purple.

They jumped up and down, laughing

because their trick had worked.

The mothers did not laugh.

"Evan!" said his mother, still pale.

"I thought you would know better

than to play a trick like that."

Abe and Sarie's mother, her basket

of berries spilled at her feet,

said soberly, "Abe, never, never do

such a thing again! You know

the Indians have always been our friends."

Even Sarie knew they had made a big
mistake. Without a word they all
helped pick up the spilled berries.
On the way home, Abe's mother was quiet.
"Abe," she said after a while,
"I think you are old enough to know
how it is. Some settlers cheat the
Indians and help themselves to the
Indians' land. The Indians are angry
and there's going to be trouble."
It was hard to believe.
Abe's father and Evan's father, Sam,
often visited the Indians in their
villages. They were friends.
"From the beginning," Mother recalled,
"the Indians invited the white settlers
to share the land with them—to eat out of
the same bowl, they said. But many of the
settlers aren't satisfied. They want

the whole bowl."
So that's how the trouble started,
thought Abe. Just to think about such
greedy guests made him furious.

At home, Abe scrubbed his face in the creek.
He carried in wood for the night.
Trouble! As he smelled the good
corn bread on the table,

it did not seem possible.

Sarie came in holding tightly to
a bowl of raspberries.

She set it down next to the corn bread.

Father came in with fresh milk
and they all sat down to supper.

Chapter Two
Abe Decides

Next day Abe was helping build a lean-to
for their new goats.
They had bought the goats from neighbors
who moved back to where they came from.
Father went for some rope.
He was gone for a long time.
Abe was tired of cutting evergreen branches

for the goat-shed roof.
He went to get a drink from the
water bucket outside the cabin door.
He heard his father inside saying:
"You make it sound like life or death."
"That's just what it is," replied Mother.
"Things couldn't be much worse."
"We could let him decide for himself,"
said Father.
"You know he's too young for that,"
objected Mother.
Abe dropped the dipper back
into the bucket with a splash. To his
parents' surprise he walked in the door.
"I'm not too young." Abe stood as tall
as he could. "I'll decide."
"Oh?" said Father.
"What would your decision be?"
"That depends," replied Abe. He had

no idea what they were talking about.
Whatever it was, he wasn't going to
spoil his chances with questions.
Mother and Father seemed upset,
but they went on talking.

"The Shawnees wanted me to bring
my boy along," said Father.

"But that was in better times,"
replied Mother. "Nobody knows
who his friends are anymore."

"Yes," Father agreed. "That's why
we have to work harder than ever
at understanding each other."
Father always had his own way of
looking at things.

Mother said sadly, "I know you
believe that to go see the Shawnees
now may save lives. But most other
people think the opposite. They say

you can't trust the Indians.
Even Sam won't go with you anymore."
"I have an idea!" spoke up Abe.
His parents seemed taken aback,
as if they had forgotten he was there.
"The Shawnees won't be afraid of
someone my age," Abe went on sensibly.
"They know Father wouldn't bring me
along if he was looking for trouble."

Mother looked at Abe like she did
when she was measuring him for a
new pair of pants.
"Let him decide," she said.
"Do you know it's almost a half day's
walk each way?"
"Yes, I know," replied Abe.
"What do you want to do?" asked Father.
"I always wanted to visit the Shawnees,"
said Abe. "And now I have my chance!"

The next morning Mother got up before
dawn and made a big breakfast of
barley cakes, raspberries, milk, and cheese.
It was still partly dark when
Abe and his father started out.

They were not alone in the forest.
The birds and animals were rustling about
at their morning business. When the sun
got warm, the forest became still except
for the buzz of insects. The birds and
animals had found cool places to rest.
Abe would have liked to do the same,
but they had to keep walking.
Right now he would have liked to sit down
under a big tree with the Indians,

like William Penn in the almanac.
He kept looking for a Shawnee as they
walked on the long trail beneath the trees.
"We meet, we meet on the path of goodwill. . ."
William Penn's words were running through
Abe's head, keeping time with his numb feet.
He walked along in a daze.

When at last an Indian appeared and
led them to his village, it was just as Abe
had dreamed it would be.

In the Shawnee shelter of boughs,
it was shadowy and cool.
When Abe and his father arrived,
the Shawnees were gathered inside,
around a large pot of cooked pumpkins.
The Indians welcomed their two visitors
and made room for them to sit down.
The Shawnees gave Abe and Father
large oak leaves for plates and
mussel shells for spoons.

As they all ate together from the pot,
Father talked with the Indians
in their own language.
Around the Shawnees' earth table,
trouble seemed far, far away.
Abe nodded off to sleep while
the Indians and Father talked together.
Father woke him when it was time to leave.
The trail seemed even longer than
in the morning. When they came to
a spring along the way, they stopped
for a cool drink and a short rest.
Then they started off again.
It was late afternoon, and there
was only one thing to do, no matter
how tired they were—keep on walking.
When they finally reached home,
Abe was so tired he couldn't even
remember going to bed.

Chapter Three
Thunder in the Night

Sarie woke up suddenly in the dark.
"What's that?" she whispered,
punching her brother to wake him.
"Just thunder. Let me sleep,"
grumbled Abe.
There it was again!
The thunder stopped, right in
front of their door.
That was not thunder. Sarie covered
her head. But Abe heard voices.
He climbed out of bed,
down the ladder from the loft.

29

Below, the room was dark and empty.
Abe heard the voices outside, and
looked through the crack
of the open door.
His father and mother were talking
to someone, but it was too dark to
see at first who it was.
The man was standing by a horse and

a loaded wagon.

"You too, Sam?" Abe's father asked
him sadly. Now Abe knew who the man
was. It was Evan's father.
Their friends were huddled together on
the seat of their wagon.
Abe's father was putting a gun
into Evan's father's hand.

"Would you keep this gun for me,
since you are determined to go?" asked
Abe's father. "It would be foolish to
keep it here at a time like this.
They do not trust us anymore."
Abe's eyes went up to the empty pegs
above the door where their gun had hung.
He wondered why his father was giving
it away. How could they hunt now?
The wagon with Evan's family in it
thundered on down the road.
Abe stepped out into the moonlight

and stood by his father.

"What is wrong? Where are they going?"
he asked.

"They are on their way to the army
headquarters at Fort Harrison,"
Father told him.

"Abe, I must tell you. The Indians
have been pushed too far.
They have burned the next village.
Our people are afraid. All night long
they have been leaving the settlement.
Everyone is gone but us."

"Shouldn't we leave too?" asked Abe.

"Our neighbors think so. What do
you think?" his father asked him as
they went back into the cabin.
Abe knew that their family had
always been at peace with the Indians.
Still, would Indian strangers know that?

"We have no way to protect ourselves,"
Abe said. He looked at the empty pegs
above the door where the gun had been.

His father saw him.

"We don't need that," said Father.

As far as he was concerned, everybody in
the world was God's family.

That included Indians.

"But would it hurt just to go to
Fort Harrison until the trouble
blows over?"

Abe looked at his father and at his mother,
who was standing by the fireplace
wrapped in an old quilt.

"The guns at Fort Harrison are there
to get rid of Indians, one way or another,"
Father said.

"Guns don't talk our language," said Mother.

The next days were lonely with
everyone else gone to Fort Harrison.
No one called to Abe and Sarie.
The only ax that rang in the clearing
was their father's.
The only chimney with smoke curling
from it was their own.

The dark empty windows in the
other houses looked like blind eyes.
When Abe looked down the road
at those windows, he felt
lonely and afraid. No one was left,
no one but themselves.

Chapter Four
Surprise Visit

One day Mother was busy baking biscuits.
Father was cutting wood.
Abe and Sarie were stacking it by
the fireplace.
All at once a flock of chattering
blackbirds flew up at the edge
of the clearing.
A strange Indian stepped out of the forest,
then another Indian and another.

Soon many Indians in war paint were
coming in a line toward the cabin.
They did not look to the right nor
to the left.
They carried knives and tomahawks.

39

Father laid down his ax and hurried
to meet them. Abe could not move.
His mother stood at the door
with Sarie behind her.
Father greeted the Indians.
He held out both his hands and said,
"Good day, friends!"

The Indians stopped. They looked down
at his empty hands, but said nothing.
They looked in the door.
"Welcome!" said Mother in a small,
strange voice.

The leader of the Indians brushed
past her, into the house.
The others followed.

"Guns!" demanded
the leader gruffly.
His tall black and
white feathers
touched the ceiling.
"No guns here," said
Father. "Go and see."
He waved his hand
toward the cupboards
and the loft.

The Indians padded all around the room.
They peered into the cupboards.
They climbed the ladder to the loft.
Mother moved quietly to the fireplace.
While the visitors watched,
she took hot biscuits from the fire.

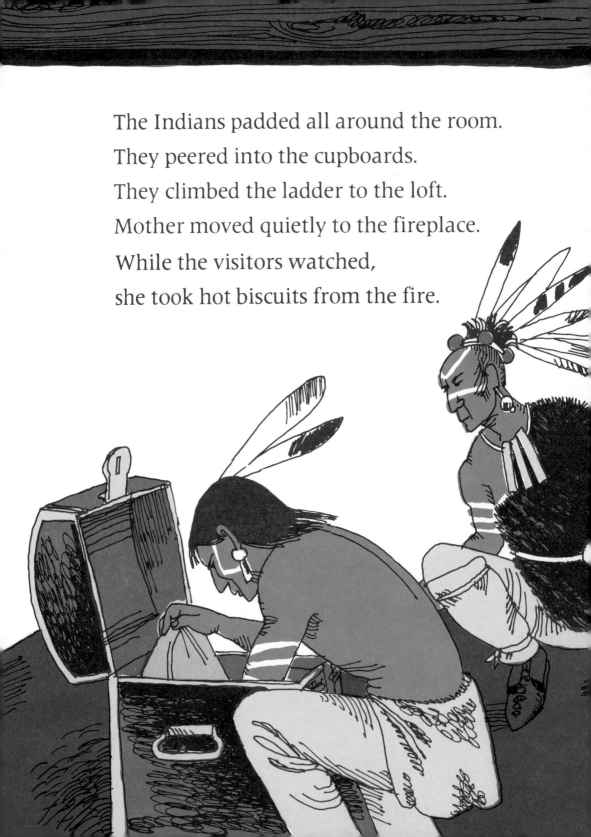

"Abe," said Mother, "please fetch
the molasses from the shelf."
The Indians watched
every move he made.
Abe put the crock of molasses
on the table beside the biscuits.
"Welcome. Help yourselves,"
said Father.

49

The visitors crowded around the table.
The leader reached for a biscuit.
It was food he was not used to.
He dipped the biscuit into the
molasses. The others did the same.
Crumbs fell on the table.

Molasses dripped on the floor.
As the men moved around the sticky floor,
their moccasins made a smacking sound.
When the biscuits were all gone,
the Indians left as quickly as
they had come.

But at the edge of the forest
they stopped and sat down in a
circle on the ground.
"Are the Indians tired, Father?"
asked Sarie.
Father took her hand in his.
He did not answer.
He was watching.

The Indian chief stood up in the
middle of the circle. He talked firmly
and pointed toward the cabin.
The other Indians answered in a low
chorus. Whether in anger or not,
who could tell?
All the Indians became silent for
a moment. They made no move.

Then their leader sprang toward the cabin.
Something long and thin as a knife
flashed in his hand.
Abe huddled close to his father.
As the Indian came nearer, Abe saw
what he was carrying.

It was a long white feather.
When the tall Indian reached them,
he stopped. He stuck the white feather
above the doorway where they stood.
He said something. It sounded like
"Good day . . . friends."

Abe looked up at the feather
above the doorway.
It was the long white plume from
the chief's headdress.
When Abe turned again,
the Indian was gone.
With the others, he had disappeared
into the forest.
Mother sank down on the doorstep
with a deep sigh.
"The Indians do understand,"
said Abe.
"They know
we are their friends."

"As long as the white feather is
above our door, all the Indians who
pass this way will understand," said Father.
"A white feather is the Indians'
sign of peace."

ABOUT THE STORY

In the early days of North America there were
many ways of life among the settlers, just as there
were many different tribes of Indians. Some pioneers
never helped themselves to Indian lands or used guns
against them. The only weapons they trusted were
fairness and confidence toward their Indian
neighbors.

A warring chief was asked why one such
settlement was never attacked, while others around it
were being destroyed. He replied, "We warriors
meddle with a peaceable people? That people, we
know, will not fight. It would be a disgrace to hurt
them."

The White Feather is based on the experience of a
Quaker family in the settlement of Cincinnati, Ohio,
about 1812. The official name for Quakers then, as
now, is Friends.